Dear Parent:
Your child's love of reading starts here!

Every child learns to read in a different way and at his or her own speed. Some go back and forth between reading levels and read favorite books again and again. Others read through each level in order. You can help your young reader improve and become more confident by encouraging his or her own interests and abilities. From books your child reads with you to the first books he or she reads alone, there are I Can Read Books for every stage of reading:

SHARED READING
Basic language, word repetition, and whimsical illustrations, ideal for sharing with your emergent reader

BEGINNING READING
Short sentences, familiar words, and simple concepts for children eager to read on their own

READING WITH HELP
Engaging stories, longer sentences, and language play for developing readers

READING ALONE
Complex plots, challenging vocabulary, and high-interest topics for the independent reader

ADVANCED READING
Short paragraphs, chapters, and exciting themes for the perfect bridge to chapter books

I Can Read Books have introduced children to the joy of reading since 1957. Featuring award-winning authors and illustrators and a fabulous cast of beloved characters, I Can Read Books set the standard for beginning readers.

A lifetime of discovery begins with the magical words **"I Can Read!"**

Visit www.icanread.com for information on enriching your child's reading experience.

A GREEN, GREEN GARDEN

BY MERCER MAYER

HARPER
An Imprint of HarperCollinsPublishers

To Eileen and Tom Hearn

I Can Read Book® is a trademark of HarperCollins Publishers.

Library of Congress catalog card number: 2010928921
ISBN 978-0-06-083562-0 (trade bdg.) — ISBN 978-0-06-083561-3 (pbk.)
Typography by Diane Dubreuil 16 17 18   SCP   10 9 8 7 6 5 4   ❖   First Edition
A Big Tuna Trading Company, LLC/J. R. Sansevere Book
www.littlecritter.com

It is time to plant
my garden.

We go to the garden store.

It has everything we need.

I want a green, green garden.
I find many seeds to plant.

Mom says, "We will buy some seeds."

Dad says, "We will also buy some baby plants."

They are very little.

They all look the same.

Dad rents a plow
from Mr. Pinky.

We go home to plant my
green, green garden.

Dad plows the garden.
We pick up stones
and clumps of grass.

14

This is not fun.

We plant the seeds
and the baby plants.

I am tired. I need cool water.

We are finished.

I say, "Now we can rest."

Dad says,

"We must water each plant."

We take turns.

Every day we weed,
water, and wait.

We weed, water, and
wait some more.

We wait a lot.

Dad takes pictures.

At school I learn more
about gardening.

We make a compost heap
full of old leaves and stuff.
It makes good garden dirt.

We buy worms
to put in my garden.

We buy good bugs
that eat bad bugs.

Deer come and eat some
of my garden.

Blue wants to protect it.

Finally, I have
a green, green garden.

I have a yellow, orange,
and red garden, too!

We have a great dinner, all
from my green, green garden!